parents and caregivers,

Stone Arch Readers are designed to provide enjoyable reading experiences, as well as opportunities to develop vocabulary, literacy skills, and comprehension. Here are a few ways to support your beginning reader:

- Talk with your child about the ideas addressed in the story.

- Discuss each illustration, mentioning the characters, where they are, and what they are doing.

- Read with expression, pointing to each word. You may want to read the whole story through and then revisit parts of the story to ensure that the meanings of words or phrases are understood.

- Talk about why the character did what he or she did and what your child would do in that situation.

- Help your child connect with characters and events in the story.

Remember, reading with your child should be fun, not forced. Each moment spent reading with your child is a priceless investment in his or her literacy life.

GAIL SAUNDERS-SMITH, PH.D.

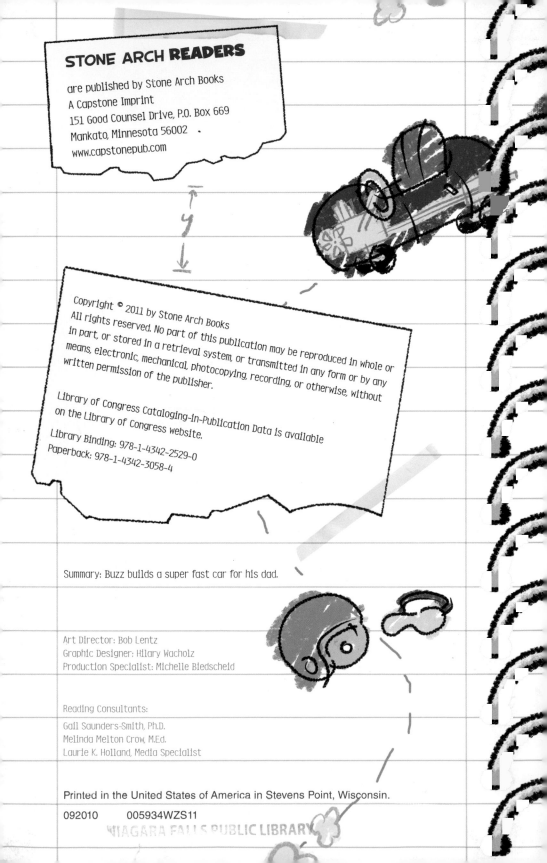

STONE ARCH **READERS**

are published by Stone Arch Books
A Capstone Imprint
151 Good Counsel Drive, P.O. Box 669
Mankato, Minnesota 56002
www.capstonepub.com

Library of Congress Cataloging-in-Publication Data is available
on the Library of Congress website.

Library Binding: 978-1-4342-2529-0
Paperback: 978-1-4342-3058-4

Summary: Buzz builds a super fast car for his dad.

Art Director: Bob Lentz
Graphic Designer: Hilary Wacholz
Production Specialist: Michelle Biedscheid

Reading Consultants:

Gail Saunders-Smith, Ph.D.
Melinda Melton Crow, M.Ed.
Laurie K. Holland, Media Specialist

Printed in the United States of America in Stevens Point, Wisconsin.

092010   005934WZS11

BUZZ BEAKER
AND THE
SUPER FAST CAR

Written by
CARI MEISTER

illustrated by
BILL McGUIRE

STONE ARCH BOOKS
a capstone imprint

Buzz Beaker loves
to make cool new stuff.
He keeps his ideas in a
special notebook.

Dr. Beaker is Buzz's
dad. He likes to invent
things, too.

Buzz's dog, Raggs, is
always excited for new
inventions.

Buzz Beaker liked to go fast.
He ran fast.

He rode his bike fast.

He skated fast.

Buzz loved fast roller coasters.

Buzz loved fast cars.

Buzz wanted to go fast all of the time. But there was a problem.

His dad was very, very slow.

Dr. Beaker walked slowly.

He mowed the lawn slowly.

And worst of all, Dr. Beaker
drove his car very, very slowly.

Buzz was late for everything.
He was late for his baseball
game.

He was late for his tuba lesson.

He was even late for his own birthday party.

One day, Buzz asked his dad,
"Can we go faster?"

Dr. Beaker just shook his
head. "Sorry, Buzz," he said.
"I like to go slow. It helps me
think."

Buzz frowned. He watched
Raggs race the car home.

Raggs won.

"I must do something!" Buzz said to himself.

Buzz sat down on the stump to think. He watched Larry race by on his bike. He watched Sarah fly by on her roller skates.

"See," he said. "Everybody likes to go fast."

Buzz jumped up.

"I know!" he said. "I will make a car that only goes fast. Then my dad can't go slow. He will see how much fun it is to go fast."

Buzz drew his plans.

Then he went to work.

Buzz worked and worked.

He had a few problems along
the way. Sometimes the car
parts ran away from him.

Buzz kept working. Soon he fixed the problems.

He was ready to show his dad.

"Dad!" said Buzz. "Will you be the test driver?"

"Of course!" said Dr. Beaker. He was very excited.

Buzz gave his dad a helmet
and a padded suit.

"Do I really need this?"
Dr. Beaker asked.

"Get in!" said Buzz.

Dr. Beaker put on his seat belt.
Buzz showed him the controls.

"Just push that button," said
Buzz.

"Okay!" said Dr. Beaker.

Dr. Beaker pushed the button.
The car started. It zoomed!

"By the way," yelled Buzz, "it only goes fast. It is impossible to go slow in my fast car."

Dr. Beaker raced through the
neighborhood.

He raced through the park.

He even raced through the
lake. Buzz's car was very fast.

At first Dr. Beaker was
worried. After all, he had spent
his whole life going slow.

Soon Dr. Beaker forgot his
worry. He liked going fast. He
loved going fast!

He could still think. He just
thought faster.

When the car ran out of gas,
Dr. Beaker got out.

"That was awesome!" he said.

Now Buzz has a different problem.

They are early for everything!

THE END

STORY WORDS

roller coasters   impossible

excited   neighborhood

helmet   awesome

Total Word Count: 427

LOOK WHAT BUZZ IS BUILDING!